The Smile Shop

A book to share from
Scallywag Press

First published in Great Britain in 2020
by Scallywag Press Ltd, 10 Sutherland Row, London SW1V 4JT

Text and illustration copyright © Satoshi Kitamura, 2020
The rights of Satoshi Kitamura to be identified as the author and illustrator
of this work have been asserted by him in accordance with the
Copyright, Designs and Patents Act, 1988

Printed on FSC paper in China by Toppan Leefung

001

British Library Cataloguing in Publication Data available
ISBN 978–1–912650–21–7

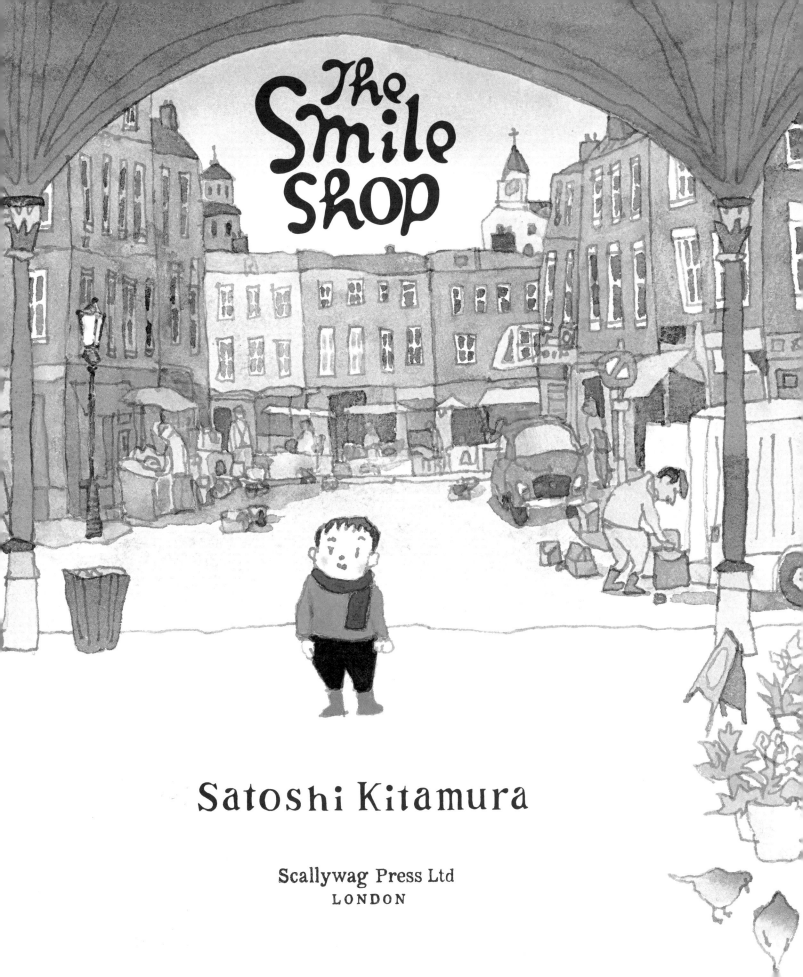

The Smile Shop

Satoshi Kitamura

Scallywag Press Ltd
LONDON

I'm so excited!

I have saved all my pocket money
and today I'm going to buy myself
something for the very first time . . .

The market
is very
busy . . .

There are so many shops and stalls,
and such wonderful colours . . .

and tempting smells!

That apple pie looks tasty . . .

I wonder which clock is telling the right time . . . ?

Oh, what a beautiful
little boat! It's quite
expensive, though . . .

Wow! I can make a sound!

I like this hat! It suits me
down to the ground . . .

Now I must decide
what to buy.

What? Oh no!

My money has gone down the drain!

Only one
coin is left . . .

I haven't enough to
buy anything now.

'SMILE'?

Is this a smile shop?

Do they sell *smiles* here?

A smile is probably what I need,
although I don't feel like smiling . . .

'Excuse me,' I say to the man
behind the counter. 'I have
very little money but could
I buy a smile, please?
A little one, perhaps?'

'I'm afraid we don't sell
smiles here, Sir,' he replies.

'But I thought you were
a Smile Shop,' I whisper.

'Well, we call ourselves Smile,' the man goes on,
'but a smile is not something that money can buy.
A smile is something you can only –'

He stops talking
and stares at me.

And then . . .

'A smile is something you can
only exchange and share!'
And he smiles a big smile.

So I smile, too!

The man takes
a picture of
me smiling
and gives
me the photo.

Then we exchange smiles
again and wave goodbye.

And I see the street is smiling.
Everyone is smiling.
The whole world
is smiling . . .

. . . with me.